The Princess
AND THE *Giant*
A TALE FROM SCOTLAND

Retold by Suzanne I. Barchers
Illustrated by Marie Lafrance

RED
CHAIR
·PRESS·

Please visit our website at **www.redchairpress.com**.
Find a free catalog of all our high-quality products for young readers.

 For a free activity page for this story, go to
www.redchairpress.com and look for Free Activities.

The Princess and the Giant

Publisher's Cataloging-In-Publication Data
(Prepared by The Donohue Group, Inc.)

Barchers, Suzanne I.
The princess and the giant : a tale from Scotland / retold by Suzanne I. Barchers ;
illustrated by Marie Lafrance.
 p. : col. ill. ; cm. -- (Tales of honor)
Summary: After the king dies, the queen and her three daughters must leave the castle and work
hard to survive. However, when a giant steals from their garden and then kidnaps the daughters,
one of the captured princesses must use ingenuity and perseverance to help them escape. Includes
special educational sections: Words to know, What do you think?, and About Scotland.
Interest age level: 006-010.
ISBN: 978-1-937529-77-2 (lib. binding/hardcover)
ISBN: 978-1-937529-61-1 (pbk.)
ISBN: 978-1-936163-93-9 (eBook)
1. Creative thinking--Juvenile fiction. 2. Perseverance (Ethics)--Juvenile fiction. 3. Princesses--
Juvenile fiction. 4. Giants--Juvenile fiction. 5. Folklore--Scotland. 6. Creative thinking--Fiction.
7. Perseverance (Ethics)--Fiction. 8. Princesses--Fiction. 9. Giants--Fiction. 10. Folklore--Scotland.
I. Lafrance, Marie. II. Title.

PZ8.1.B37 Pr 2013

398.2/73/09411   2012951563

This series first published by:
Red Chair Press LLC   PO Box 333   South Egremont, MA 01258-0333

Printed in the United States of America

1 2 3 4 5 18 17 16 15 14

*L*ong ago, the king of Scotland died. His cousin, a jealous man, inherited the throne. The new king sent the widowed queen and her three daughters to a remote country cottage. They could take one cow and their clothes with them. As for food, they would have to survive on what they could grow in their garden.

The queen was hardworking and courageous. Once they were settled, she gathered her daughters. "Our first job is to gather stones from the moor. We must build a wall to keep the cow out of our garden. Let's get started."

4

Months later, the middle daughter went to the garden to get a cabbage. She ran back crying, "Mother! Come look! Someone has taken a whole row of cabbages!"

They all rushed out to the garden.

"Don't be upset, daughters," their mother said. "More cabbages will grow in time."

The youngest daughter looked around and said, "Mother, look! There are huge boot prints by the wall."

"Only a giant could make such huge prints!" cried their mother.

The girls were angry about their hard work going to waste.

"I will stay out tonight and watch for that giant!" declared the oldest daughter. And that night she hid herself in the garden.

As the moon rose, she saw a huge giant stepping over the wall. He bent his large body toward the ground and began to cut off cabbages.

"Why are you stealing our cabbages?" the girl asked.

The surprised giant said, "What is it to you?"

"They are ours! Leave our garden!" cried the girl.

The giant did leave. But first he plucked her like a flower and popped her into his sack of cabbages.

Once they arrived at the giant's house, the oldest daughter climbed out of the sack.

"Get to work," the giant directed. "Start by driving the cow to pasture. Then make the porridge and clean the wool."

Later, trying to clean the wool, the girl heard a knock at the door. "Who's there?" she asked.

"A traveler in need of a bite to eat," came the reply.

"Leave or face the wrath of a giant!" she cried. By the time the giant returned, she had ruined the wool and burned the porridge. Furious, he tossed her into the loft.

That night, the middle daughter waited up for the giant. She intended to make him give back her sister. But he spotted her, tossed her into the sack, and then picked the cabbages. By the time they arrived at his home, she was nearly smothered.

He set her to work cooking and cleaning.
Just like her older sister, she made a mess of
it. He tossed her into the loft, where the sisters
hugged each other in relief.

That night, the giant found the youngest daughter sitting on the garden wall.

"Good evening, giant," she said. "I am ready to go with you."

The giant was impressed with her manners. He picked his cabbages and then set her in the sack. She had a small pair of scissors in her pocket and used it to cut a small hole in the sack. She watched the way to his house, cheerfully stepping out of the sack on their arrival.

"In the morning, drive the cow to the pasture. Make the porridge. Then comb, card, and spin the wool. Do you think you can do that?" asked the giant.

"I will do my best," she answered. Later, she heard a knock at the door. She greeted a strange little fellow with red hair and blue eyes. He looked to be lost and starving.

"Please," she said, "take my porridge."

After he had eaten his full, the man saw the wool and said, "Let me repay your kindness."

After spinning a beautiful length of white wool, he turned and disappeared.

The giant was delighted when he returned, saying, "Your work is good. Take the ladder, and you can visit your sisters in the loft."

The next morning, the youngest sister gave the
giant his breakfast and begged a favor.

"Please, sir, there is no one left to help my
mother. Would you take her a basket of heather
for the cow's bed?"

The giant was quite charmed by her and
agreed. Soon he was on his way and she went
back to work. That night, he once again praised
her work.

The next morning, the youngest sister asked another favor.

"Please, sir, would you take this basket of grass to my mother for fodder for the cow?"

The giant cheerfully lifted the basket and carried it right to her mother. He came back to a sparkling house, saying, "Tomorrow you can let your sisters come down and help you."

"That will be wonderful," the girl replied. "But I have another favor to ask of you. Tomorrow, would you take this basket of myrtle to my mother? She would be so grateful if you could get it to her early."

The giant agreed.

Early the next morning, he lifted the basket to his shoulder and went to the cottage. He set it by the garden and left.

The youngest daughter got out of the basket and ran to the cottage, greeting her mother and joining her sisters that the giant had unwittingly carried home. After many hugs, they sat down to breakfast.

Just then, a messenger from the king knocked at the
door. The king, who had a change of heart, invited
the queen and her daughters to return to the palace.

They finished their meal, gathered their
belongings, and climbed into the waiting coach.

As for the giant, he expected to find the three sisters hard at work. Instead he found a cold fire in an empty house. He rushed back to the queen's cottage where he could not find the sisters or a single cabbage. The queen and her daughters had carried away every last one.

courageous: brave; to not be afraid of danger

moor: an unplanted open field or marsh

unwittingly: not done on purpose; happens by accident

widowed: to be left alone due to a woman's husband dying

Question 1: Why did a queen and her three daughters live in a cottage and grow cabbages in a garden?

Question 2: What happened to the princesses when they stayed out to catch the cabbage thief? Did the third daughter go willingly with the giant? Why?

Question 3: The giant gave chores to each princess. How did the giant feel when he came home after the third princess was to do her jobs?

Question 4: How did the youngest princess trick the giant? What happened when he carried the baskets of grass and heather to the queen's cottage?

About Scotland

Scotland has a rich history of myths and legends. Centuries ago superstition was widespread in this country of mysterious castles, foggy moors, and deep lakes. Unusual events were often explained by invented stories and tales. These were passed on by word of mouth and added to with colorful new details about monsters, giants, and goblins.

About the Author

After fifteen years as a teacher, Suzanne Barchers began a career in writing and publishing. She has written over 100 children's books, two college textbooks, and more than 20 reader's theater and teacher resource books. She previously held editorial roles at Weekly Reader and LeapFrog and is on the PBS Kids Media Advisory Board. Suzanne also plays the flute professionally – and for fun – from her home in Stanford, CA.

About the Illustrator

Montreal-based Marie Lafrance has been drawing illustrations for most of her life. She has drawn pictures for magazines, posters, billboards, and board games. But illustrating books for young readers is her passion.